# After HAPPILY —EVER— AFTER

SAVE the FOREST!

## The Ugly Duckling Returns

After Happily Ever After is published by Stone Arch Books
A Capstone Imprint
1710 Roe Crest Drive
North Mankato, Minnesota 56003
www.capstonepub.com

First published by Orchard Books, a division of Hachette Children's Books
338 Euston Road, London NW1 3BH, United Kingdom

Library of Congress Cataloging-in-Publication Data is available
on the Library of Congress website.

ISBN-13: 978-1-4342-7953-8 (hardcover)
ISBN-13: 978-1-4342-7959-0 (paperback)

Summary: It's been a while since the Ugly Duckling turned into a Swan, and
life has been good. Now he's a famous model, but does being the biggest
celebrity in the Forest mean he can't help save it?

Designer: Russell Griesmer
Photo Credits: ShutterStock/Maaike Boot, 4, 5, 51

Printed in China.
092013    007737LEOS14

# After HAPPILY —EVER— AFTER

## The Ugly Duckling Returns

by TONY BRADMAN

illustrated by SARAH WARBURTON

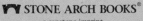
STONE ARCH BOOKS®
a capstone imprint

So the Ugly Duckling
survived the bullying,
turned into a beautiful swan,
and lived happily ever after.
And then ...

"Can you see him yet?" yelled one of the gaggle of giggling goose girls hanging around outside Forest TV.

They were being held back by a line of
security guards. "I think I'll die if he doesn't
come soon!"

Just then, an elegant figure appeared
at the studio door. All the goose girls were
screaming with excitement and waving like
crazy. Even the security guards were looking
over their shoulders, their mouths open in
wonder.

"Give us a smile, Swan!" yelled a troll with a camera. A crowd of reporters had appeared, pushing and shoving each other and taking lots of pictures.

"Of course," said the elegant figure, and he smiled. Hundreds of camera flashes went off. Several of the goose girls swooned from the excitement.

The elegant figure laughed, climbed into his limo, and was swept away. He relaxed in the luxurious leather seat and shook his head in amazement.

How strange it was to have crowds waiting everywhere he went, and to hear them calling him Swan.

After all, he still thought of himself by the name he had been given when he had first hatched out of his egg — the Ugly Duckling.

Life had certainly changed for him since those days. Everybody had been horrible to him then.

They had made fun of his big head, his
stubby brown feathers, and his clumsy walk.

But he had grown up to be a beautiful swan. In fact, he had turned out to be so good-looking he had become a model.

Now he was the biggest celebrity in the Forest. He appeared on TV, and his picture was in all the magazines.

Things were good for the Ugly Duckling, and he hoped they were going to stay that way. He would hate going back to being the way he had been before. He shuddered at the thought.

Suddenly he realized the limo had stopped. He looked out of the window and saw they were in a line of cars. "What's the problem, driver?" he asked.

"Too many cars. Total traffic jam," muttered the driver, honking the limo's horn. "The traffic in the Forest is terrible, and it's getting worse every day."

Now the Ugly Duckling felt depressed, and also a little guilty. Life might be good for him, but there was a lot wrong with the world.

His driver was right. There was far too much traffic in the Forest, and the pollution was awful.

Nobody seemed to care, though, and that worried the Ugly Duckling. By the time he finally got home to his fabulous mansion hours later, he had decided he wanted to do something about it. But what?

That night he looked through the local paper, brooding. A tiny item caught his attention.

Some locals had started a new anti-pollution campaign called Save The Forest! They were planning to have a rally the very next day, and the Ugly Duckling decided he would go.

He disguised himself so he wouldn't attract attention, and stood at the back of the crowd. After he listened to all the speeches he approached Rapunzel, who was one of the organizers of the event.

"Hello," he said. "I was wondering if I could do anything to help?"

"Yes, please. We could always use another volunteer to hand out leaflets," said Rapunzel.

Then she paused, and looked at him a little more closely. "Hang on," she murmured, her eyes growing wide. "I don't believe it! You're Swan!"

The Ugly Duckling's heart sank, but he didn't need to worry. The other organizers recognized him too, but they were all just pleased to meet him. The Ugly Duckling asked how the campaign was going.

"Not very well so far," Rapunzel said. The others nodded. "We can't seem to get any real publicity. Forest TV told us we're not exciting enough."

Suddenly the Ugly Duckling had an idea. "Maybe I could have a word with them," he said. "They're always asking me if I want to do something special."

"Could you really?" asked Rapunzel. "That would be absolutely wonderful."

The Ugly Duckling went to see his contacts at Forest TV the very next day.

He told them about how important the Save The Forest! campaign was, and explained that he wanted to help his new friends get lots of publicity.

He agreed to speak at the next rally and hoped that Forest TV would cover it. The Forest TV trolls seemed very excited and promised they would, but the Ugly Duckling didn't stop there.

He visited all the magazines and newspapers in the Forest. He made them promise to send their reporters to the rally as well.

That evening, he biked over to see
Rapunzel in her palace. He had given up
being driven around in a limo now that he
realized it was bad for the Forest.

"Wow, that's great!" said Rapunzel
when the Ugly Duckling told her what
he had done.

Rapunzel and her team worked very hard for the next couple of days getting everything ready for the rally.

They rented a hall in the center of the
Forest and set up booths where people
could get information or volunteer for the
campaign.

The Ugly Duckling stood in the wings of the stage waiting for the rally to begin. He was scheduled to give the first speech, and he was feeling happy and excited.

At last, they opened the doors. A huge crowd stampeded in, trampling over the booths in a wild rush to get to the stage. There were TV trolls, dozens of reporters, and lots of fans, including the usual gaggle of giggling goose girls.

"Give us a smile, Swan!" the reporters yelled, pushing and shoving each other. It was a complete disaster, and the Ugly Duckling was horrified.

"I'm sorry, Rapunzel," he said later, when they were cleaning the hall. "I don't seem to have been much help after all. Quite the opposite, in fact."

"Well, thanks for trying," Rapunzel said sadly. "I suppose we'll just have to keep thinking. There must be some way we can get our message across."

That night, the Ugly Duckling sat watching TV in his mansion and brooding again. He was really fed up. Once upon a time he had desperately wanted to be beautiful. But now it seemed that being good-looking wasn't any use at all.

Nobody had been interested in what he wanted to say. The reporters and fans only cared about what he looked like.

The campaign still wasn't getting any publicity, and that meant the Forest was becoming more polluted every day. Suddenly, he sat up.

Maybe he could shock everyone into seeing things differently! He called Rapunzel and told her his plan.

"I like it!" said Rapunzel, and laughed. "If that doesn't work, nothing will!"

A few days later, Rapunzel announced
that Save The Forest! would be holding
another rally, and that Swan would be
there.

TV crews, reporters, and fans flocked to
the same hall, but this time the curtains
were drawn across the stage.

And when they were pulled back, they didn't reveal Swan. Instead, they revealed the Ugly Duckling! Everybody gasped!

It had taken a lot of effort with makeup and false feathers, but he had managed to make himself appear like his old self.

"This is the way I used to look," he said. "But we're making the Forest look just as ugly because of all the pollution we create. We can't go on ignoring it."

It was a huge success, of course.
Everybody listened to his speech, and
to all the speeches that followed.

The Save The Forest! campaign got the publicity it needed, and the Ugly Duckling soon went back to being Swan.

The gaggle of goose girls still swooned when he smiled, but he decided he could live with that.

Because of the Ugly Duckling, everyone in the Forest joined the Save The Forest! campaign and lived HAPPILY EVER AFTER!

THE END

## ABOUT THE AUTHOR

**Tony Bradman** writes for children of all ages. He is particularly well known for his top-selling Dilly the Dinosaur series. His other titles include the Happily Ever After series, *The Orchard Book of Heroes and Villains*, and *The Orchard Book of Swords, Sorcerers, and Superheroes*. Tony lives in South East London.

## ABOUT THE ILLUSTRATOR

**Sarah Warburton** is a rising star in children's books. She is the illustrator of the Rumblewick series, which has been very well received at an international level. The series spans across both picture books and fiction. She has also illustrated nonfiction titles and the Happily Ever After series. She lives in Bristol, England, with her young baby and husband.

# GLOSSARY

**brooding** (BROOD-ing) — worrying or thinking about something

**campaign** (KAM-payn) — a series of actions organized over a period of time in order to win something

**celebrity** (suh-LEB-ruh-tee) — a famous person

**gaggle** (GAG-guhl) — a flock

**leaflets** (LEEF-lits) — sheets of paper giving information or advertising something

**pollution** (puh-LOO-shuhn) — harmful materials that damage the air, water, and soil

**publicity** (puh-BLISS-uh-tee) — information about a person or an event that is given out to get the public's attention

**rally** (RAL-ee) — a large meeting

**swooned** (SWOOND) — fainted from excitement

## DISCUSSION QUESTIONS

1. Were you surprised when Swan changed himself back into the Ugly Duckling for the big rally? Why or why not?

2. Do you think the Ugly Duckling should go by his original name or officially change it to Swan? Explain your answer.

3. Talk about an organization or club you are involved with. Why do you like being a part of it?

# WRITING PROMPTS

1. Write a paragraph about your favorite celebrity.

2. Make a list of at least five things you can do to help save Earth.

3. Write a newspaper article about Swan and the Save the Forest! organization and rally.

# THE FUN DOESN'T STOP HERE!